The Wheels on the...Uh-Oh!

Sue Tarsky
pictures by Alex Willmore

Albert Whitman & Company
Chicago, Illinois

The wheels on the bus go
'round and 'round,
'round and 'round,
'round and 'round.
The wheels on the bus go
'round and 'round,

all through the...

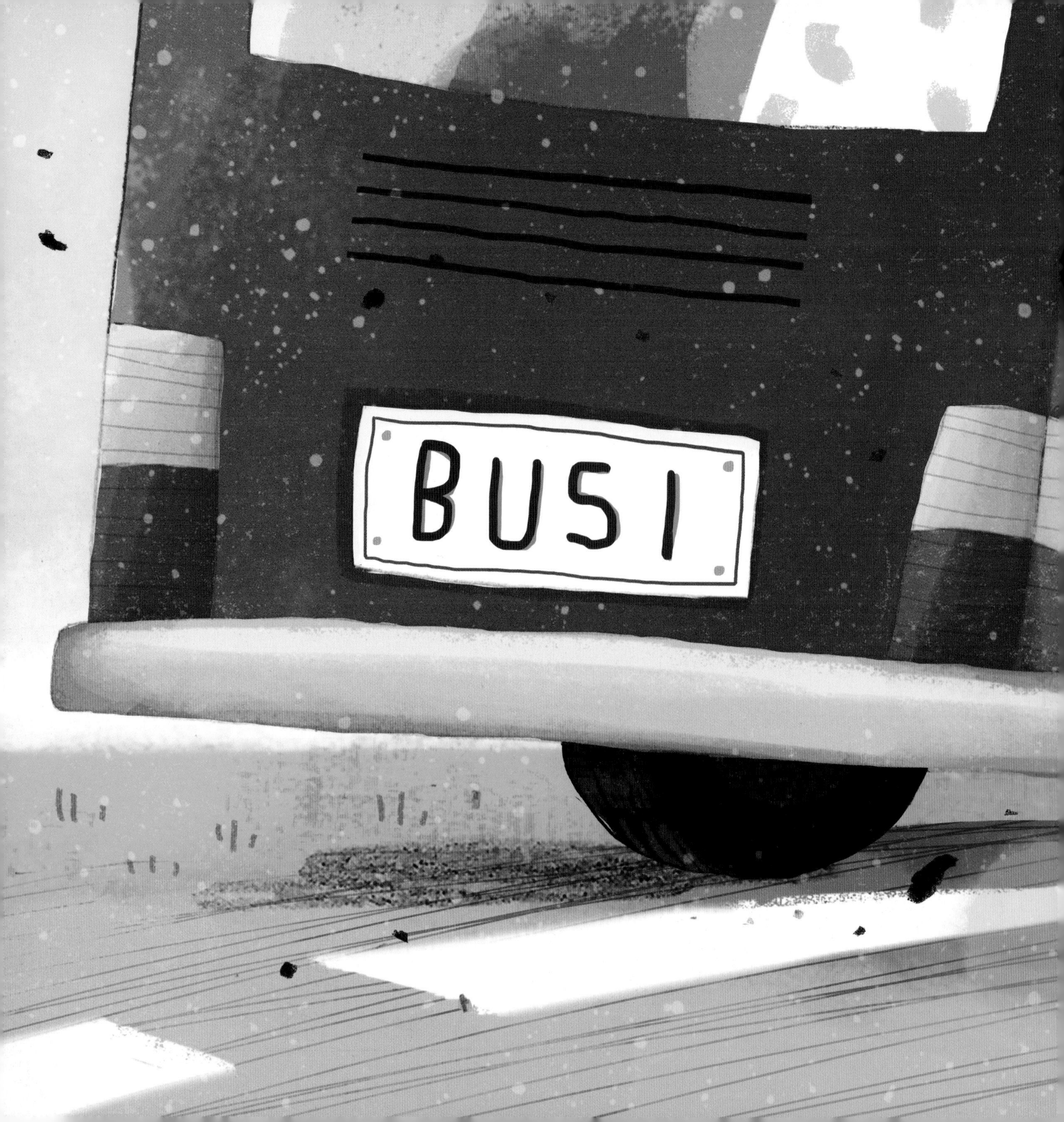
BUSI

The driver on the bus says,
   "Off, off, off...
   off, off, off...
   off, off, off!"
The driver on the bus says,
   "Off, off, off...

everyone off the bus!"

The policeman comes to tell them,
   "Move this bus,
   move this bus,
   move this bus!"
The policeman comes to tell them,
   "Move this bus,

please move it now!"

The riders from the bus go,
"Grumble, grumble, groan,
grumble, grumble, groan,
grumble, grumble, groan."
The riders from the bus go,
"Grumble, grumble, groan,

grumble, groan and moan!"

The driver gives the wheel a
    push, push, shoooove,
    push, push, shoooove,
    push, push, shoooove.
The driver gives the wheel a

push, push, shoooove...

The wheel from bus goes
bump, whizz, roll...
bump, whizz, roll...
bump, whizz, roll.
The wheel from the bus goes
bump, whizz, roll...

right down the road!

The riders from the bus shout,
"Stop that wheel!
Stop that wheel!
Stop that wheel!"
The riders from the bus shout,
"Stop that wheel!"

All through the town.

The digger stops the wheel with its

    scoop, scoop, scoop,

    scoop, scoop, scoop,

    scoop, scoop, scoop.

    The digger stops the wheel with its

    scoop, scoop, scoop,

just like that!

The driver checks the wheel and
adds a patch,
adds a patch,
adds a patch.
The driver checks the wheel and
adds a patch,

the wheel's okay!

Now everyone helps to
push and click,
push and click,
push and click.
Now everyone helps to
push and click...

"We've all fixed the wheel!"

The driver on the bus says,
"On, on, on,
on, on, on,
on, on, on!
We're going on a picnic,
and we'll all have fun—

everyone on the bus!"

with love and thanks to the best brother
and sister-in-law in the world, Fred and Sue—ST

For Dara and Bump—AW

Library of Congress Cataloging-in-Publication data is on file with the publisher.

Text copyright © 2018 by Sue Tarsky
Pictures copyright © 2018 by Albert Whitman & Company
Pictures by Alex Willmore
First published in the United States of America in 2018 by Albert Whitman & Company
ISBN 978-0-8075-8869-7

Printed in China
10 9 8 7 6 5 4 3 2 1 WKT 22 21 20 19 18

For more information about Albert Whitman & Company,
visit our website at www.albertwhitman.com.